THE WONDROUS SEED

TAHIR SHAH

MAHYA SADEGHI

THE WONDROUS SEED

TAHIR SHAH

MAHYA SADEGHI

MMXXIII

Secretum Mundi Publishing Ltd
124 City Road
London
EC1V 2NX
United Kingdom

www.secretum-mundi.com
info@secretum-mundi.com

First published by Secretum Mundi Publishing Ltd in
Daydreams of an Octopus & Other Stories, 2022
Published in this edition, 2023

THE WONDROUS SEED

Artwork drawn by Mahya Sadeghi

A CIP catalogue record for this title is available from the British Library.

ISBN 978-1-914960-97-0

VERSION 22032023

Visit the author's website:
Tahirshah.com

Once upon a time, before the great continents had risen from the seas, there was an island known by its inhabitants as Pop-tica-pie.

Little more than a tiny speck of dry land in an endless expanse of blue, it was a paradise.

The people who lived there had no contact with anyone else, but they were the happiest folk you could ever hope to meet.

They spent their days in the forest or down at the water's edge, or at the ancient altar which was in between the two.

The people of Pop-tica-pie sang and laughed all day long, and when they slept, they smiled.

No one there ever wondered whether they were the happiest people in all the world… because they assumed they were the only people in existence.

Once in a while, what looked like an object would be seen far in the distance, the size of a pea running the length of the horizon.

When such an object was spotted, the people would gather at the great altar and sing a song in honour of the ancestors for revealing a little magic to amuse them.

No one on the island went without food or fresh water. They fashioned themselves clothing from the fibres of palm fronds and, when the summer storms raged, they would cluster together at the altar, singing a song of wonder and woe.

On a day much like any other, a little boy called Salap went down to the water's edge to search for shells.

He was kind, thoughtful, and the apple of his parents' eyes. If there was anything that singled him out from the other boys, it was his inquisitive nature.

So, Salap was paddling in the water looking for shells when he spotted something bobbing up and down.

Curious as to what it might be,
he waded out, grabbed the object,
and hurried back to the beach.

Squatting on the sand, Salap examined it.
It was unlike anything he had ever seen before.

As wide as his torso, it was wooden, curved, and wonderfully alluring.

Unsure what to do, Salap carried it up the beach and to the home where he lived with his parents in the shade of the great palm tree.

Within ten minutes a crowd had gathered, everyone wishing to see the peculiar object that little Salap had found.

One at a time, they leaned forward and touched it, laughing and singing with delight.

'It was sent to us by the ancestors as a musical instrument. Listen how it rattles when it's shaken!' an old woman cried out.

‘It’s a float to use in fishing!’
yelled someone else.

‘No, no,’ corrected a third, ‘it’s a throne on which the leader of the island must sit!’

All day, the people of Pop-tica-pie chattered, laughed, and sang about the object that Salap had discovered in the sea.

And all night long,
each one of them imagined
what they would use it for.

The morning after the curious object had been discovered, the man who had assumed it was a float grabbed it and ran out into the water with it to show the others.

The ancient who had thought it was an instrument yelled out that the fisherman had stolen it.

Then, the man who thought it was a throne snatched it away from the fisherman.

Positioning it close to the altar,
he sat down on it and sang triumphantly.

By nightfall, the island's harmony was lost.

Everyone, from the smallest child to the oldest and most wizened crone, wanted to have their time with the object.

Accordingly, a rota system was drawn up, in which everyone – irrespective of gender or age – was permitted a few minutes with the object.

Despite good intentions, the system caused infighting right from the start.

Everyone, it seemed, accused everyone else of taking too long when it was their turn.

As the days of the rota progressed,
the people of Pop-tica-pie began
treating the object too roughly.

One of the little boys dropped it against a rock and the outer covering of fibrous husk fell away.

All the people came together in sorrow.

For the first time in as long as anyone could remember, the laughter and the singing ceased.

The people of the island were truly sad that their beloved object, the one thing which had brought universal delight and joy, was damaged.

Calling everyone to the altar, the leader of the community ordered that they would do what they always did in times of uncertainty.

They would ask the ancestors for advice.

And so, as the sun slipped down below the horizon and dusk fell, every mouth whispered a plea to the ancestors, asking what to do with the magical object from the sea.

All night, the people of
Pop-tica-pie whispered…

…and all the next day…

…and through the next night…

Then, as dawn broke over the horizon, something happened which was witnessed by everyone.

A little mouse burrowed up out of the sand and scampered into the undergrowth beyond the beach.

His lungs filling with air, the head
of the community cried out:
'See that – a sign! See the sign
sent by the ancestors!'

‘What does it mean we should do?’
asked the oldest crone.

'It means we must bury the object in the ground,' said Salap, the boy who had discovered it in the first place. 'Because if it's buried, then no one can damage it, and it can continue towards its own destiny.'

Every man, woman, and child spoke at once – quizzing, questioning, cooing, and demanding.

As their noise grew louder than anything the island had ever experienced, the head man raised a hand in the air.

'Salap was the person who found the object,' he said, 'so it should be Salap who decides. If he thinks the mouse was a sign that we must bury the object sent by the ancestors, then that is what we shall do!'

A spade was brought out and a spot at the edge of the forest was chosen.

With everyone crowding around, Salap dug a hole and placed the object into it.

Before it was covered up with soil, each member of the community was allowed to reach forwards and touch it one last time.

Weeks passed.

Then months.

After almost a year, Salap was wandering up from the beach with some shells he had found when he spotted something at the edge of the forest…

…something that had not been there before.

A little green shoot…

…a little green shoot growing straight up.

Calling out as loudly as he could,
Salap announced what he had seen.
Instantly, everyone clustered around.

The oldest crone rubbed a thumb
to each eye and gasped.
'It was a seed!' she exclaimed.
'A seed sent by the ancestors!' the others sang.

Many more months passed.

The shoot grew and grew…

…and grew and grew…

Up…up…up…

And as it grew, the people of Pop-tica-pic
would cluster around and sing songs
to the plant, or rather, the tree.

Because that's what the seed had grown
into – a magnificent though very
odd-looking palm… quite unlike
any other on the island.

On some nights when the summer storms raged and the people clustered together to sing, they would take it in turns to remember the time when the mysterious object was found by the little boy, Salap – the little boy who was now a grown man.

They would remember how they all fought because they loved the object, and because they wanted to make use of it.

And they would remember that only
by planting it did they come to realize
it was in actual fact a seed…

…a seed that, by growing into a tree, could be loved and celebrated by all.

Many more years passed.

Eventually, Salap had great-grandchildren.

One afternoon, as they waded through
the shallows in search of shells, one of them
called out on their way back from the sea.

‘Look! Look!’ she cried.

All the people of Pop-tica-pie
clustered around.

‘What’s wrong?’

'Look up at the magical tree… the one you all talk about all the time!'

Every face looked upwards.

Then, every mouth gasped.

You see, high above the tree's trunk were
a clutch of coconuts growing, just like the
one Salap had found as a boy.

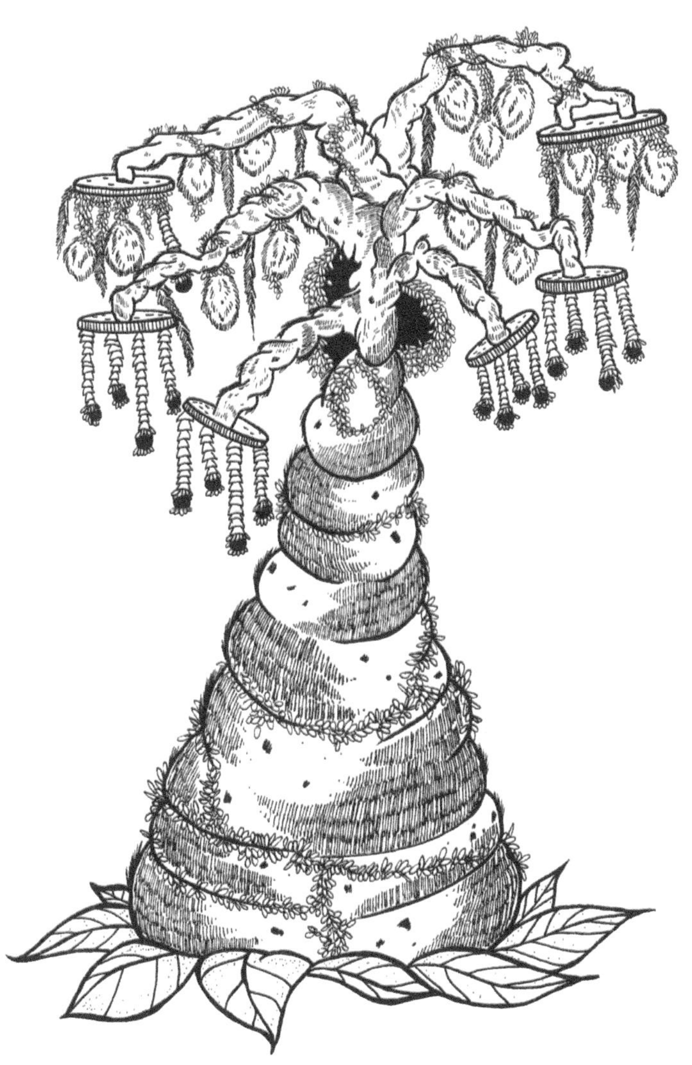

With time, the coconuts grew to maturity
and they were planted in the forest,
so that they could reach their destiny
and cause no jealousy.

And when those seeds grew into palms
and had coconuts of their own, some
were planted and others were taken
into the waves and released.

So that they could travel over oceans
and give joy to others across the seas.

Finis

About the Author

Descended from a long line of storytellers, writers, and savants, Tahir Shah is one of the most prolific authors of his generation. He has published more than sixty books in numerous genres, including travel, fiction, and fantasy, as well as tales for children.

Raised in the tradition of Eastern 'teaching stories', Shah is passionate about stories and storytelling. He regards the ability to learn from folklore as being in us all, what he calls a 'default setting of humankind'. As well as having written scores of books, Shah has made documentaries for National Geographic TV and The History Channel. He is the founder and CEO of the charity, The Scheherazade Foundation.

About the Artist

Mahya Sadeghi was born in Iran. She studied IT and worked as a UI designer until 2016, when she decided to follow her childhood dream of becoming an artist. Mahya's passion lies in Persian miniatures, taking particular inspiration from the great Iranian painter and illustrator, Sani ol-Molk. She now works as a freelance artist on projects in Iran, Sweden, and the UK.

Books By Tahir Shah

Travel

Trail of Feathers
Travels With Myself
Beyond the Devil's Teeth
In Search of King Solomon's Mines
House of the Tiger King
In Arabian Nights
The Caliph's House
Sorcerer's Apprentice
Journey Through Namibia

Novels

Jinn Hunter: Book One – The Prism
Jinn Hunter: Book Two – The Jinnslayer
Jinn Hunter: Book Three – The Perplexity
Hannibal Fogg and the Supreme Secret of Man
Hannibal Fogg and the Codex Cartographica
Casablanca Blues
Eye Spy
Godman
Paris Syndrome
Timbuctoo

Nasrudin

Travels With Nasrudin
The Misadventures of the Mystifying Nasrudin
The Peregrinations of the Perplexing Nasrudin
The Voyages and Vicissitudes of Nasrudin
Nasrudin in the Land of Fools

Teaching Stories

The Arabian Nights Adventures
Scorpion Soup
Tales Told to a Melon
The Afghan Notebook
The Caravanserai Stories
Ghoul Brothers
Hourglass
Imaginist
Jinn's Treasure
Jinnlore
Mellified Man
Skeleton Island
Wellspring
When the Sun Forgot to Rise
Outrunning the Reaper
The Cap of Invisibility
On Backgammon Time
The Wondrous Seed
The Paradise Tree
Mouse House
The Hoopoe's Flight
The Old Wind
A Treasury of Tales
Daydreams of an Octopus & Other Stories

Miscellaneous

The Reason to Write
Zigzag Think
Being Myself

Research

Cultural Research

The Middle East Bedside Book

Three Essays

Anthologies

The Anthologies

The Clockmaker's Box

The Tahir Shah Fiction Reader

The Tahir Shah Travel Reader

Edited by

Congress With a Crocodile

A Son of a Son, Volume I

A Son of a Son, Volume II

Screenplays

Casablanca Blues: The Screenplay

Timbuctoo: The Screenplay

A REQUEST

If you enjoyed this book, please review it on your favourite online retailer or review website.

Reviews are an author's best friend.

To stay in touch with Tahir Shah, and to hear about his upcoming releases before anyone else, please sign up for his mailing list:

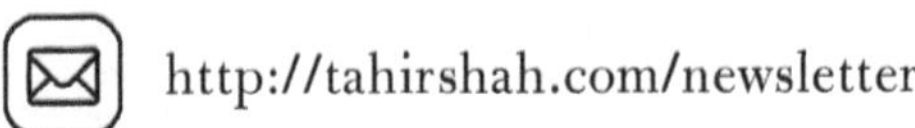
http://tahirshah.com/newsletter

And to follow him on social media, please go to any of the following links:

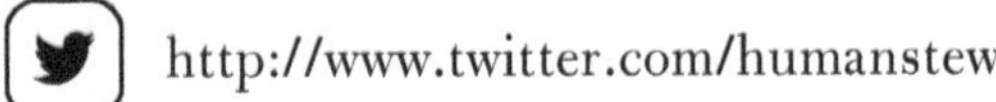
http://www.twitter.com/humanstew

@tahirshah999

http://www.facebook.com/TahirShahAuthor

http://www.youtube.com/user/tahirshah999

http://www.pinterest.com/tahirshah

https://www.goodreads.com/tahirshahauthor

http://www.tahirshah.com

www.ingramcontent.com/pod-product-compliance
Lightning Source LLC
Chambersburg PA
CBHW030522310726
48979CB00010B/1772/J

* 9 7 8 1 9 1 4 9 6 0 9 7 0 *